Closed Legs Don't Get Fed 2

Reds Johnson

Closed Legs Don't Get Fed 2
Copyright © 2015 by Reds Johnson
Interior Design Formatting | Strawberry Publications, LLC

ISBN-13: 978-1722714970
ISBN-10: 1722714972

One

"**S**orry about that. Derrick called to let me know the date has to be cut short," Chelsea said as she gulped down her glass of wine.

"I paid ten fuckin' grand to be with you. Fuck that," Jeremy barked.

"Well, that's not my problem. Daddy's rules are daddy's rules. Now, can you please take me back?" Chelsea said as she headed to the door.

Jeremy was fuming. His hands were shaking and his palms were sweaty. He took out a little plastic baggy that contained a white, powdery substance. Jeremy then took his pinky fingernail, got some out and snorted it up each nostril. He cracked his knuckles and swiped everything off of the table and walked out. Everyone looked shocked by what he just did. Jeremy got in the car and slammed the door hard.

"You wanna be with this nigga, then cool," Jeremy said as he sped off.

"You need to slow down. I can't believe you're acting like this," Chelsea said.

Jeremy sped in and out of traffic. His mind was in a thousand places at once. He was seeing three of everything. Everything seemed to be moving all at once. Jeremy was starting to hear voices, so he began banging on his head with his fist.

"Get the fuck out of my head," he yelled.

"Pull over right now, Jeremy. Let me out of this damn car," Chelsea said in a frightened tone.

Jeremy ignored her and kept on going. He sped past a police car and they put on their sirens and followed. Jeremy only stopped because he had reached his destination. Once he saw Derrick's car, the emotions started flowing and he became angry all over again. As Chelsea opened the car door and proceeded to get out, Jeremy grabbed a handful of her hair and slit her throat.

"If I can't have you, then nobody can!"

***

Jeremy couldn't take what he had done to Chelsea. Months went by and it was still eating him up inside. He never intended to hurt Chelsea, but he was so upset that she chose his son over him. In just a short period of time, Jeremy had fallen in love with Chelsea. He couldn't forgive himself for what he'd done. Jeremy knew that there was only one thing to do.

He sat in front of the Philadelphia Police Department and stared into space. Jeremy thought about how much wrong he had done in his life. After abandoning his son Derrick and his ex-wife Demetria, Jeremy used all of his life savings on drugs. He became a nobody, and that's just how his son treated him. Like he was nobody.

Jeremy got out of his 1986 Cadillac Deville. The walk into the police department seemed like an eternity to Jeremy. A policewoman behind the glass eyed Jeremy suspiciously. He walked over to the lady behind the glass and spoke with pride.

"My name is Jeremy Robinson, and I am turning myself in for the attempted murder of Chelsea White."

Two

Chelsea was sitting in a small two-bedroom apartment. After Chelsea relapsed, she met up with an old friend of hers name Ace. Ace was a wannabe at its finest. He was 32 years old and he was the black sheep of the family. Not to mention he wasn't easy on the eyes, standing at five feet even with the skin complexion of the midnight sky without the stars. His teeth overlapped and he was slightly cross-eyed. Ace was an ex-crackhead who swore he was coming up in the world.

"See, Chelsea, if you would've kept in contact with me, you wouldn't even be in this situation," Ace stated.

Chelsea rolled her eyes because she knew he was no better than her. They were both junkies, and even though Ace claimed he was clean, everyone else knew the truth.

"Ace, save it, because I would be in the same position that I'm in now if I still dealt with your ass," Chelsea confirmed.

Ace ignored her and lit up his black and mild. He and Chelsea lost contact when she was 23. They only reconnected because he saw her walking down the street asking people for change.

"Don't try to put me down. Shit, I'm doing alright for myself. Whatever happened to Mr. Goody Two Shoes, hmm? What's his name? Jason, that's it," Ace shot back.

Whenever Chelsea heard Jason's name, she became emotional. She wished she was the one with him instead of Sarah. Chelsea knew she had taken advantage of Jason, but she expected him to take her back once again like he always did.

"Don't you worry about Jason. He's doing fine. He's taking care of our child just until I get myself together," Chelsea stated.

Ace laughed as if Chelsea had said that funniest thing on Earth.

"Yeah, yeah, yeah. I know he's marrying some sexy-ass black woman named Sarah. I heard you went there trying to get him back, but he booted you right the fuck out," Ace revealed as he took another pull of his black.

Chelsea shot daggers at Ace. Even though his story was false, she still wanted to know how he knew about Sarah.

"How do you know about Sarah?" Chelsea said.

Ace knew he had her.

"Don't worry about all of that. Just know when the time comes, you will find out everything you need to know," Ace boasted.

Three

Everyone and they mama knew Ace would never be anything in life. No one believed in him except one person: his brother Sincere. Sincere was the handsome one. He was 6'1" with smooth, dark chocolate skin and very muscular. Sincere wore shoulder-length dreads with blonde tips. He could brighten up any room with his smile. He did his best to help his brother, but his help was never good enough.

"Wassup? I've been calling you for weeks," Sincere said when his brother walked up.

"A nigga been busy. I mean, I gotta work for mines. Shit just doesn't get handed to me," Ace barked.

"The fuck that's supposed to mean? I work for everything I got," Sincere shot back.

"Nigga, fuck you, you ain't work for shit. You sit around like you a fuckin' king or something. You from the hood, just like the rest of us," Ace told him.

Sincere knew things were going to go somewhere that they didn't need to go. He didn't understand why there was so much hate toward him from his brother. All he ever did was try to help him through his addiction. He never acted as if he was better than Ace, or anyone for that matter, because he grew up in the hood and hustled just like everyone else. The difference between Sincere and everyone was he hustled to get out of the hood, not to stay in it. After Sincere saved up enough, he moved out of Newark and moved to Hopewell, New Jersey. He started a construction business and was financially stable ever since. Sincere had a beautiful wife named Yana and a handsome 15-year-old son, Sincere Jr. A lot of people were jealous of Sincere for having so much, and he was only 34 years old. All Sincere wanted to do was help and give back.

"Look, bro, I turned all that negative shit into a positive, and that's the same thing I want you to do," Sincere said.

"Oh, so watchu playing daddy now, tryna tell me how to live ma life and what I should be doing? Fuck outta here," Ace told him.

Sincere counted backward from 10 before he spoke. He felt like wringing his brother's neck, but he was learning to control his temper.

"Ace, I'm willing to pay for your rehab and give you a job. All you gotta do is lose that I-don't-give-a-fuck attitude," Sincere explained.

"Rehab? Motherfucker, I been clean," Ace said.

"Oh, I guess I got *stupid* written across ma forehead. Ma nigga, you was clean. You act like I don't know you relapsed," Sincere admitted.

Sincere could tell Ace wanted to do more than talk. He didn't want to take it there, but he was more than prepared if he decided to take it there. Before either of them could say another word, his wife Yana pulled up in her all-white 2013 Benz. Sincere Jr. got out of the car first and ran over to his father.

"Hey, dad. Man, you missed a great game today. I scored 52 points! Man, they wasn't ready for me on the court today," Sincere Jr. said excitedly

"That was only a pre-game, baby boy. Don't worry, I won't miss the next one," Sincere replied.

Sincere Jr. ran into the house without even speaking to his uncle Ace. As Yana stepped out of the car, Ace couldn't help but lock eyes on her freshly-shaved chocolate legs. Yana wore a white spaghetti-strapped shirt and a pair of dark blue denim shorts that looked like they were painted on. She had a fresh pedicure, which looked beautiful in her diamond bezel sandals.

Now, Yana was Sarah's sister. They were thick as thieves. If you had a problem with Sarah, then you had a problem with Yana.

"Hello, Ace," she greeted.

"Yeah, what up, Yana? I see ma brother got you lookin' like new money," he told her.

"Excuse me?" she said as she cocked her head to the side.

"Sweetie, pay him no mind," Sincere told her.

Yana did as she was told and proceeded to walk over to her husband. She put an extra swish in her step when she walked by Ace. When she got to Sincere, her lips met his and they shared a passionate kiss. Ace rolled his eyes out of jealousy.

"Look, man, I'm out. I'll check y'all out anotha time," Ace said as he turned to walk away.

"I can give you a ride," Sincere said as he began to walk off of the porch.

"Nah, man, I caught the bus here and I can catch it back. Besides, you too good to have something like me sittin' in one of ya nice-ass rides. I'll holla," Ace said and walked away.

All Sincere could do was shake his head in disappointment.

Four

errick decided that the Miami life was treating him well. Tiffany was now his bottom bitch. She was making him crazy money, and her nickname in the streets was Deep Throat Queen.

"*Yo, Tiffany! Get ya dumb ass down here,*" Derrick yelled.

Tiffany slowly sashayed down the stairs. Her beautiful brown skin tone glistened from the body shimmer she had on. Tiffany wore her blonde and black hair up in a high bun. Although she was average, she still got the job done.

"You need to take them fuckin' cat eye contacts out. Niggas ain't liking that shit at all. You scaring away money, and I don't need that shit," Derrick barked.

Tiffany rolled her eyes. She had no idea when she befriended Derrick that he would treat her as a hoe.

Tiffany had dreams, and she was still in college. This was something she didn't have time for, and it was degrading. She was now the city whore, and wherever she went men looked at her like she was nothing but a whore.

"Derrick, I can no longer let you treat me this way. Since I've been dealing with you, I have lost every bit of confidence I've had," Tiffany explained.

Derrick chuckled. He didn't take Chelsea seriously, so he didn't understand why Tiffany thought he would take her serious.

"So, what you saying? You saying you done with me?" Derrick wanted to know.

Tiffany took a deep breath before responding.

"Yes, Derrick, I am done with you. I am going back to school, and I'ma continue to reach my goals and turn my dreams into reality. It's bad enough I have to fight for my respect," Tiffany stated.

Derrick rubbed his mustache and nodded his head up and down.

"Cool, you're free to go," Derrick told her.

Tiffany was relieved. She didn't think it would be this easy, but she was glad it was. As she turned around to leave, Derrick charged her from behind.

They fell to the floor, and Derrick repeatedly slapped her.

"Stupid bitch! You think I'ma just let you leave? Fuck no! You not going nowhere! You gon' shut the fuck up and make my money," Derrick screamed.

Tiffany's face was burning and her nose was bloody. This was not the life she expected at the age of 21. She only moved to Miami to further her modeling career, but she now knew that when her mother told her it was a bad idea, she should've listened.

Five

It was Wednesday afternoon, and Chelsea was in her bedroom getting high. This was the only thing that kept her calm since she and Jason ended. As Chelsea lit her glass pipe, she heard a big bang that made her jump. She was already high, so she thought it was the drugs that had her going crazy.

"Who is it?" Chelsea called out.

The only thing she had in her hand was a flip-flop, as if that was going to protect her.

"Why the fuck you hiding? And why you ain't got no food in this damn house?" Ace complained as he slammed the cabinets.

Once Chelsea heard Ace's voice, she calmed down a bit. She still had the jitters from the high she had.

"There's some peanut butter and jelly in the fridge," Chelsea responded as she bit her nails.

Ace looked at her with a screwed up face.

"Bitch, is you fuckin' stupid? The fuck I look like, eating a fucking choker sandwich?" Ace barked.

"Why are you coming in here with an attitude? What pissed you off?" Chelsea asked.

Ace ignored her and pushed past her so he could go in the room.

"Damn, you smoked all the shit?" he asked.

Chelsea ran back into the room and grabbed her pipe.

"Look, I had to suck a lot of dick for this, and I'm not about to let you sit here and smoke it," Chelsea stated.

Ace was pissed. Not at Chelsea, but at his brother Sincere. He felt like Sincere was trying to play him. He was only taking his frustrations out on Chelsea because he knew Sincere was not one to fuck with.

Six

"**S**incere, you've been up all night. When are you coming to bed?" Yana asked when she walked into their study.

"I'm just thinking about Ace. I hate it when we argue," said Sincere.

"Staying up all night isn't going to change the fact that you both had a disagreement earlier. Just pray about it and move on," said Yana.

"I just need him to understand that all I want is the best for him. Just because we grew up in the hood doesn't mean we need to stay in it," Sincere explained.

Yana rubbed his shoulders before she spoke.

"You can't save someone who don't wanna be saved."

Sincere sat there lost in his thoughts. He knew his wife was right, but something inside him wouldn't let him give up on his brother.

Seven

Sarah and Yana were sitting at her kitchen table talking while Jason and baby Chelsea went out to pick up a few groceries.

"So, how is everything, baby sis?" Yana asked.

"Everything is great. Jason is a wonderful man. I'm glad that I can be his backbone through this whole Chelsea situation," Sarah explained.

Yana sipped on her tea before she spoke.

"How is that going? Like, how is he taking things now that they're officially over?" Yana asked.

"It's a process, but he's handling things very well. You can tell that she hurt him very badly. You know, she reminds me a lot of Ace. No matter how much Sincere tries to help him, he just doesn't accept it," Sarah stated.

Yana nodded her head up and down because Sarah was right on point with that one.

"Sis, you right, but you know it's not 'you don't know what you have until it's gone.' You knew what you had, you just didn't think you would lose it. And I'm pretty sure Chelsea sees that," Yana explained.

Jason came through the door with the car seat in one hand and bags in the other.

"Hey there, Yana, how are you?" Jason asked.

"Hey Jason. I'm doing wonderful. How are you?" Yana said.

Sarah took baby Chelsea out of Jason's hands and put her in the swing.

"I can't complain. My beautiful fiancée is helping me get through everything day-by-day. I couldn't have asked for anyone better," Jason said as he planted a wet kiss on Sarah's lips.

All she could do was smile because Jason knew exactly what to say so she would be smiling for the remainder of the day. Yana got up and grabbed her purse.

"Amen to that, Jason. Well, look, I'm about to get out of here. I have a lot of business to handle for Sincere, so Sarah, sweetie, I'll call you later, ok?" Yana said as she headed for the door.

"Ok sis," Sarah replied.

Jason sat down at the table, and Sarah could tell something was on his mind.

"What's wrong, love?" she asked as she sat on his lap.

"I think I saw Chelsea while I was at the market," Jason blurted.

Sarah looked at Jason, but never responded. Chelsea had been the talk of the house for the last few months, and she was tired of it. Although she and Jason were engaged, it still felt like he was with Chelsea. Sarah wondered what it would take for Jason to understand Chelsea didn't want any help. Jason didn't know it, but he was about to lose his wife before they even got married.

Eight

Ace sat in a dirty hotel room drinking a Heineken while a teenage girl from around the way name Keisha gave him head. The hotel manager had been calling his room for over an hour, and Ace refused to pick up the phone.

"Oh shit, right there," he moaned as he pushed her head down further.

"Damn, nigga, you choking me. Calm yo' ass down," Keisha said with attitude.

"Bitch, who you talkin' to? Ya raggedy-ass can get the fuck out ma room right now," Ace shot back.

Keisha wiped Ace's pre-cum off of her mouth and laughed like he had just said the funniest thing on earth.

"Nigga, you act like you doin' me a favor. Fuck outta here, you lil' dick nigga," Keisha said as she got up and started gathering her things.

Even though it was just the two of them in the room, Ace was embarrassed. He got up and walked over to Keisha and pushed her.

"Bitch, you got shit fucked up if you think I'ma let you walk outta here after you done disrespected me. You know who the fuck I am?" he said with a scowl on his face.

"Yeah, the same nigga that got caught sucking dick in the woods for a crack rock," Keisha shot back.

Ace's blood was boiling. Keisha had definitely hit him with a low blow. He grabbed his Heineken bottle and smacked her hard across the face with it. Ace then started kicking and stomping Keisha in the stomach.

"Talk shit now, bitch! Talk shit now," he cheered as he continued to stomp her.

"*Ace, stop! Get off of me!*" she screamed.

A banging on the door caught his attention.

"Who is it?" he asked.

"Sir, this is the hotel manager. I am going to need you to open this door now or I am calling the police," he said in a serious tone.

Ace knew that either way he was fucked, so he had to think of a plan. He grabbed the little bit of stuff he did have and headed to the door. He slung the door open and hit the hotel manager with a quick right, knocking him out cold. Ace hopped over him and ran like his life depended on it. He pulled out his cell and called his boy, Rock.

"Yo, man, I need you to come scoop me ASAP. I'm on New Street," Ace said as he breathed heavily into the phone.

"You in luck, ma nigga. I'm, like, five minutes away," Rock responded.

Ace was relieved when he heard that.

"Cool," Ace said, and then he ended the call.

In no more than five minutes, Rock pulled up in his beat-up black 2009 Camry. Ace hopped in and gave him dap as they pulled off.

"Wassup, man? Why you in such a panic?" Rock asked.

"Man, I had to fuck this bitch up for getting outta line with me. We was in a hotel, and the fuckin' manager came up there beastin'. I had to steal on his ass," Ace explained.

Rock shook his head as he let out a chuckle.

"Yo' ass gon' end up in jail," he told him.

"Shit. Fuck that, I refuse to go to jail over some dumb bitch. Besides, all I need to do is get ma money up so I can start ma business," he bragged.

"Nigga, what business you tryna start?" Rock asked.

"I'm tryna open me up a strip club. I love ass, so it's only right. I just need the money. And I already got a top-dollar hoe who gon' make me some crazy money," Ace explained, referring to Chelsea.

Rock got real quiet. He knew exactly where Ace could get the money from. The question was, would he be down to do it? The whole strip club thing wasn't a bad idea, and Rock wanted parts. He was tired of living with different chicks and their kids. He wanted his own place, and he needed a new wardrobe.

"I know how you can get the money," Rock said.

He now had Ace's full attention.

"How?" he asked.

"We gon' rob ya brother, Sincere," Rock said with a smile.

Ace was a little shocked by Rock's response. He didn't give a fuck about Sincere, but this wasn't his MO at all. Ace was actually afraid to go to war with his brother, considering he was well known for putting in work.

"Man, I don't know if we should do this," Ace stated.

Rock looked at him with a frown on his face,

"Ace, don't bitch up. Now is not the time for that," Rock said seriously.

Rock was in the streets all his life. There was nothing nice about him because he was always looking for a come-up. Unlike Ace, Rock was a stick-up kid, and he had been since he was a teenager. Now, at the age of 31, he still was up to his money-scheming ways. Rock wasn't a bad-looking guy, but they say a bad attitude makes anyone ugly. He was about the same height as Ace with the skin complexion of brown sugar. He was so muscular, and they called him Rock because of how big his head was.

"You know how Sincere get down. I know for a fact that this shit gon' go sour," Ace confessed.

Rock shook his head back and forth. Ace was being a coward, and Rock didn't like that at all.

"Look, nigga, you either gon' be down with it or you not. You said that you tryna make a come-up, and all you need is the money. Well, there it is," Rock stated.

Ace thought on it for a few. He knew Rock was right. Ace thought about Chelsea and how he knew she would do anything for her next hit.

Nine

A week later, Sincere took it upon himself to pay for Ace's rehab. All Ace had to do was check himself in, but he was nowhere to be found. Yana looked out of the window at Sincere as he poured himself another glass of Moet. He looked stressed, and she knew it was because of Ace. She didn't understand why Sincere still babysat his brother like they were still kids.

"How are you feeling?" she asked as she walked on their deck.

"Not good. I got a lot of tension in my neck," he told her.

"You want me to run you a hot bath?" Yana asked.

"Yes, that would be nice" he replied.

Yana headed back into the house and went upstairs. She went into their master bedroom and grabbed some candles and rose petals. Afterward, she went into the bathroom and turned on the

Jacuzzi. She figured they both could use some alone time since Sincere Jr. was away on a trip with his friends. Yana lit the candles and placed them around the bathroom. She put some rose petals in the Jacuzzi and made a trail from the bedroom leading into the bathroom. She took off her clothes and put on her silk pink robe and headed back downstairs.

"Baby, it's all ready," she said as she peeked her head out of the sliding door.

He got up and walked into the house to see Yana standing by the stairs with her robe open, holding a fresh bottle of Moet. Sincere gave her a flirtatious smile as she slowly walked up the stairs, and he followed. He followed the rose petal trail into the bathroom. Yana stood in front of him and took her robe off. Her hard, chocolate nipples stared Sincere right in the eyes. His dick got hard instantly by the sight of her chocolate body. Sincere undressed and walked over to Yana. He pulled her close, and she welcomed his tongue into her mouth.

"Mmm, it's been a few weeks since we did this," Sincere moaned.

"I know, and this is much needed," Yana said as she let him go and stepped into the Jacuzzi.

Sincere stepped in with her. Once they were settled in, Yana poured them both a half glass of Moet. She loved Sincere, and whenever he needed a stress reliever she would go all out.

"This feels good," Sincere said out loud as he sank deeper into the water.

Yana took a few sips of her Moet and then sat it on the edge of the hot tub. She went over to Sincere and began kissing on his neck. He sipped his drink with one hand and reached down and started playing with her pussy with the other hand. Yana closed her eyes as Sincere played in her juice box. He knew all of her spots.

"I need to feel you now," he said as he put down his glass and pulled Yana on top of him.

He slid his eleven-inch dick inside her with one full stroke. Sincere bounced Yana up and down on his shaft as water splashed everywhere.

"Yes, baby, right there," she moaned.

Sincere was enjoying every bit of her sweet cave as he sucked on one of her nipples.

"Turn that ass around," he demanded.

Yana lifted up and felt a quiver as his thick shaft slid out of her. She turned around and bent over the edge of the tub. He massaged his dick and then fingered her hole. She closed her eyes and reached down to play with her clit. Sincere entered her from behind and began giving her slow, deep strokes. Between the length of his dick and the pressure of the water, Yana was in heaven. She rubbed her clit at a medium pace. Sincere then pulled halfway out and roughly slammed back into her.

"*Oh fuck,*" Yana screamed.

"Yeah, you missed this dick, didn't you?" Sincere asked as he smacked her ass.

"Hell yeah," Yana told him.

"You love this dick?" Sincere asked as he pushed all the way inside her and held himself there.

"Yes, Sincere baby, I love this dick," she moaned.

"I'ma bust all in that pussy," he told her.

"Yeah, I want you to," Yana moaned as she threw her ass back and tightened up her vaginal walls, trying to force the cum out of him.

Sincere could no longer control himself. He grabbed her hips tightly and released a blast of hot cum inside of her.

"Ooh, fuck. Ooh, shit. Damn, girl, I love you," said Sincere as he slowly pulled out of her.

Yana smiled and wiggled her ass as she stood up. She reached down and stuck her middle finger in her pussy. She pulled out her cum-covered finger and stuck it in her mouth and licked off her juices. Sincere got out of the Jacuzzi and grabbed his robe. He went into the bedroom and checked his cellphone for any missed calls. To his surprise, he had a missed called from Ace. He quickly called him back.

"Yo, bro. Wassup? I seen that you called me, but I was a little tied up," Sincere explained.

"Yeah. I thought about watchu said, and I wanted to talk more about it," Ace said.

Sincere couldn't believe what he was hearing. He was so shocked that he had to look at his phone to make sure he hadn't dialed the right number. His brother was as stubborn as a mule, and the fact he actually took Sincere up on his offer was shocking.

"Damn, you serious?" Sincere asked.

"Yeah, man," Ace said as he cleaned his AK-47.

"A'ight, cool, so you can come by ma office first thing Monday morning and we can get the paperwork started. Oh, and by the way, I went ahead and paid for ya rehab. All you have to do is check yourself in. If you're going to be working for me, I need you to be clean, bro," Sincere explained.

Ace felt his eye twitch. He wanted to blow a fuse right then and there, but he didn't want to mess up Rock's plan, so he bit his tongue.

"A'ight, cool. Well, I'ma holla at you later," Ace said.

He didn't even give Sincere a chance to respond before he hung up. Sincere knew his brother way too well, and he knew he had struck a nerve by mentioning his drug habit. However, what did puzzle him was the fact he didn't react toward it.

Ten

"Shut the fuck up, bitch, and take it," Derrick demanded.

Tiffany was on all fours getting fucked in her ass by a random guy. She winced in pain as the man dry-fucked her.

"Derrick, please tell him to stop," she cried.

"I can't get ma nut off if this bitch gon' continue to cry and shit. If I don't get ma nut, you don't get paid," the guy snapped.

Derrick was getting pissed, because now Tiffany was messing up his money, and he didn't appreciate that.

"Smack that bitch and tell her to shut the fuck up," Derrick shot back.

The man took his big, ashy-black hand and went across Tiffany's face.

"Shut up, bitch. It will be over soon," the man barked.

Tears rolled down Tiffany's face as she fought to hold in her cries. This was all too much for her, and she wanted it to end. The man grabbed a handful of her hair and yanked it until he released inside of her.

"*Urgh*," he moaned.

Tiffany felt sick to her stomach as she felt his warm cum shoot up her ass. He pulled out his dick and smeared the remainder of his nut on her ass.

"A'ight, nigga, now give me ma five hundred," Derrick said with his hand out.

The man gave Derrick seven one hundred dollar bills.

"That's 200 extra for letting me smack that bitch," the guy said with a laugh as he left out.

Tiffany was still face down and ass up. She was so embarrassed.

"Why the fuck you still in that same position? Go wash ya ass because that shit is dirty", Derrick said as he walked out of the room.

Tiffany slowly got up and went into the bathroom. She looked in the mirror and wondered whom that girl was staring back at her. Tiffany wanted her old life back, and she knew the only way that could happen was if she escaped from Derrick. She didn't know how she was going to do it, but she planned on doing it soon.

Eleven

"I'm tired of this uppity nigga. I'm ready to put two in this nigga right now," Ace barked as he paced back and forth.

Rock laughed as he emptied cigarette butts into a piece of paper he had cut earlier. They were plotting in Chelsea's two-bedroom apartment. See, Rock didn't care for Sincere either, but he was just another jealous street cat. He was one of the ones that hustled back in the day, but had nothing to show for it. After seeing Sincere make something out of himself, knowing they both came from similar backgrounds burned him up inside.

"Just be patient. Friday is almost here, ma nigga," Rock told him as he lit up his homemade cigarette.

"Nah, this nigga checked me into rehab like he ma fuckin' parent or some shit. Who the fuck he think he is?" Ace said angrily.

"He thinks he better than you. Hell, he think he better than all of us, for that matter, and we need to put this nigga to sleep as soon as possible," Rock told him.

Ace sat down on Rock's mattress on the floor. His nostrils were flared and he was breathing heavily. Deep down inside, Ace was ashamed of his failure, but he was never going to admit that. He was going to keep pointing the finger at Sincere as if he was the bad guy.

"Fuck that nigga and his wife, man. Fuck ma nephew, too," Ace said in anger.

"So how much am I getting once we get the money?" Chelsea asked.

Rock looked over at Chelsea, who was walking around in nothing but a towel. He was impressed because, for a white girl, her ass was fat.

"Damn, you looking good," Rock blurted.

Chelsea looked at him as if he had said something bad.

"You wanna taste? Because it's gon' cost you," Chelsea said, getting straight to the point.

Rock thought on it for a second. He knew that Chelsea was a crack head, but she also looked good, and pussy was pussy in his eyes.

"I only got fifty on me," Rock revealed.

"Give me eighty and then we can work something out," Chelsea told him.

Rock looked at Ace, who looked back at him.

"Man, I'm not paying for no pussy," Ace said with attitude.

"Come on, man. I'm tryna see what that pussy like, bruh," Rock begged.

Ace shook his head and pulled out the last of his money.

"I only got twenty-five, but we both gotta hit it since I'm putting in ma cut," Ace stated.

Chelsea dropped her towel and walked over to Rock. She pulled down his sweatpants and pulled out his dick. Chelsea began to suck Rock's dick, and he laid his head back. Ace pulled out his dick and mounted Chelsea from behind. He gave her quick and hard pumps. Chelsea didn't moan because Ace had nothing to make her moan.

"Put some more of that dick in ya mouth," Rock demanded.

Chelsea looked him in the eyes and then swallowed him whole.

"*Fuck*," Rock moaned.

"Yo, let me see what that's about," Ace said.

Chelsea popped Rock's dick out of her mouth. She sat on Rock's dick backwards and began to suck Ace's dick. She tried her hardest to work with what he had, but it was hard. Ace's dick kept coming out of Chelsea's mouth. It became annoying to her because it caused her to do more work.

"Maybe y'all should just fuck me so we can get this over with," Chelsea said in a bored tone.

She turned around and began riding Rock. He didn't have the biggest dick either, but Chelsea could work with it. Ace, on the other hand, tried to fuck Chelsea in the ass, but his dick kept slipping out. This whole situation turned Chelsea off.

"You like this good dick, don't you?" Rock asked as he bounced Chelsea up and down.

Her titties bounced up and down, and that turned Rock on more.

"Yeah, baby, fuck this pussy good," she moaned.

At this point Chelsea was doing anything so he could cum. She wasn't worried about Ace because he had stopped and began jerking himself off. Rock gripped Chelsea's breast and squeezed tight. Chelsea grabbed his hands and rode him like she was a cowgirl.

"Cum inside of me, baby," Chelsea purred.

Rock's face started twitching. He sat up and began licking and sucking on Chelsea's titties as he stuck his middle finger in her ass.

"Oh, I'm about to nut. Oh shit, baby, here it come," Rock moaned.

He held onto Chelsea tightly as his body jerked. Chelsea didn't let him enjoy his full nut.

"Ok, you can let me go now," Chelsea told him.

Rock slowly let her go and Chelsea climbed off of him. She grabbed her money and wrapped the towel back around herself.

"So again: how much am I getting when we get the money?" Chelsea asked.

Chelsea was about her money. Sex was strictly business to her, and there was no time to catch feelings or fall in love. The streets taught her that closed legs don't get fed.

Twelve

It was 4:00 p.m. and Yana had just walked out of the bank, making a deposit for Sincere because he was at work. She got in her car and was on her way home. Yana pulled into the driveway and turned the car off. She grabbed her purse and opened the car door. Before she could do anything, she was snatched out. She tried to scream, but the person placed their hand over her mouth. They threw her in the car and sped off. Yana was now in the car with two masked men and a woman. She was scared to death.

"Please don't kill me. I'll give you whatever you want," she pleaded.

"Bitch, shut up," Rock told her.

Yana tried to open the window and scream out, but Ace grabbed her.

"Bitch, I'll blow ya fuckin' brains out," Ace threatened.

Yana was too scared to speak.

"By the way, Chelsea, meet Sarah's sister, Yana," Ace said with a smile.

Chelsea looked at Yana with hate in her eyes. This was the first time Yana had come face-to-face with Chelsea. She had heard so much about her, but she never would've thought she would be in a situation like this with her.

"Please, I'll give you anything," Yana pleaded.

Chelsea slapped Yana in the face hard.

"*You stupid bitch! I want Jason back. Could you give me that?*" Chelsea screamed.

Ace and Rock removed their masks, and Yana frowned.

"Ace, what are you doing? What is all this about?" Yana asked.

"Money, baby girl, money," Ace responded coldly.

Thirteen

s the day went on, Sincere was worried because he hadn't heard from Yana since that morning. He called her cell, but she didn't answer. When he got home, her car was in the driveway. He was a bit relieved at first. When he got in the house, he found himself getting nervous again. The house was too quiet.

"*Yana,*" Sincere called out.

"Baby, I'm in the bedroom," she told him.

Sincere could tell something wasn't right. The way Yana spoke let him know she was frightened. He pulled out his nine-millimeter Glock and slowly walked upstairs. He could sense an unknown presence. By the time he got to the bedroom, he had a gun pointed at the back of his head.

"Drop the gun, muthafucka," Rock ordered.

"Man, what the fuck is going on?" Sincere asked.

"You heard what the fuck he said," Chelsea said as she came from the side of him with her gun pointed.

Everyone and they mama knew Sincere wasn't no punk. He stood there and held his ground.

"Nigga, if you gon' shoot me, then shoot me. Never hesitate when you behind that trigger," Sincere told him.

Rock's hand started to shake. He knew how Sincere got down back in the day. He knew if he killed him, then his whole plan was for nothing, and he knew if he let him live, then Sincere was coming back for revenge. Rock pushed Sincere into the bedroom. Sincere was crushed when he saw Yana on the floor with her hands tied behind her back and a bloody nose. What hurt him the most was the person standing behind her with an AK-47 pointed to her head. It was Ace, his own brother, his flesh and blood.

"Yo, man, what the fuck is all this about?" Sincere asked.

"Muthafucka, you know what this about. Where the fuckin' money at?" Ace asked.

Sincere couldn't believe what he was hearing. His brother was willing to kill him and his wife over some money. After all he tried to do to help Ace, it still wasn't enough. At that point Sincere realized he had to fight fire with fire, because the man standing in front of him was no longer his brother. He was his enemy.

"I don't have time for this shit. Where is the fuckin' money?" Chelsea asked.

"Baby, that's Chelsea, the girl Jason use to deal with. Ace told her I am Sarah's sister, and that's why she's here," Yana blurted out.

Sincere looked at Chelsea and then back at his brother. He was staring into the eyes of two people who were here for two things: money and revenge.

Fourteen

"You know, this is some real fuckin' shit, Ace. All I ever did was try to help you, and this is how you repay me?" Sincere stated.

"Shut the fuck up, you bitch-ass nigga. You always thought you were betta than me, so everything that's happening now, you had it coming, playboy," Ace responded.

Sincere looked at Yana, who was crying crocodile tears. As he watched his brother point that gun at her, it showed him the ultimate betrayal. They were no longer family, and it hurt Sincere more than anything, because all he tried to do was help Ace. Chelsea didn't really know what she was into. All she knew was that there was money involved.

"Get that fuckin' gun up off ma wife, yo," Sincere barked.

Ace cocked his gun, letting Sincere know he was serious. Rock and Chelsea were actually surprised by his sudden courage. It made them nervous, because they didn't plan on killing anyone, but it was clear Ace had other plans.

Fifteen

"**S**orry about that. Derrick called to let me know the date has to be cut short," Chelsea said as she gulped down her glass of wine.

"I paid ten fuckin' grand to be with you. Fuck that," Jeremy barked.

"Well, that's not my problem. Daddy's rules are daddy's rules. Now, can you please take me back?" Chelsea said as she headed to the door.

Jeremy was fuming. His hands were shaking and his palms were sweaty. He took out a little plastic baggy that contained a white, powdery substance. Jeremy then took his pinky fingernail, got some out and snorted it up each nostril. He cracked his knuckles and swiped everything off of the table and walked out. Everyone looked shocked by what he just did. Jeremy got in the car and slammed the door hard.

"You wanna be with this nigga, then cool," Jeremy said as he sped off.

"You need to slow down. I can't believe you're acting like this," Chelsea said.

Jeremy sped in and out of traffic. His mind was in a thousand places at once. He was seeing three of everything. Everything seemed to be moving all at once. Jeremy was starting to hear voices, so he began banging on his head with his fist.

"Get the fuck out of my head," he yelled.

"Pull over right now, Jeremy. Let me out of this damn car," Chelsea said in a frightened tone.

Jeremy ignored her and kept on going. He sped past a police car and they put on their sirens and followed. Jeremy only stopped because he had reached his destination. Once he saw Derrick's car, the emotions started flowing and he became angry all over again. As Chelsea opened the car door and proceeded to get out, Jeremy grabbed a handful of her hair and slit her throat.

"If I can't have you, then nobody can!"

***

Jeremy couldn't take what he had done to Chelsea. Months went by and it was still eating him up inside. He never intended to hurt Chelsea, but he was so upset that she chose his son over him. In just a short period of time, Jeremy had fallen in love with Chelsea. He couldn't forgive himself for what he'd done. Jeremy knew that there was only one thing to do.

He sat in front of the Philadelphia Police Department and stared into space. Jeremy thought about how much wrong he had done in his life. After abandoning his son Derrick and his ex-wife Demetria, Jeremy used all of his life savings on drugs. He became a nobody, and that's just how his son treated him. Like he was nobody.

Jeremy got out of his 1986 Cadillac Deville. The walk into the police department seemed like an eternity to Jeremy. A policewoman behind the glass eyed Jeremy suspiciously. He walked over to the lady behind the glass and spoke with pride.

"My name is Jeremy Robinson, and I am turning myself in for the attempted murder of Chelsea White."

Sixteen

"**S**incere, you got five fuckin' seconds to give me what I fuckin' came for," Ace threatened.

Sincere wasn't going to go out without a fight. The way Rock was shaking when he held the gun in Sincere's face showed him he wasn't built for this. Sincere quickly reached his hand back and knocked the gun out of Rock's hand. They tussled on the floor for the gun and Sincere's strength overpowered Rock's. He grabbed the gun, and with no hesitation and shot Rock in his head.

Pow.

When he turned the gun to his brother, out of fear of what would happen next, Ace blew the back of Yana's head off.

Boom.

Sincere froze in his tracks. Seeing his wife's brains splattered everywhere sickened him.

Chelsea's mouth dropped open. Their plan had gone left, and she didn't know what to do.

"I — I didn't mean to do that, bro. I'm so sorry," Ace pleaded.

Ace was already an enemy to Sincere, so Sincere didn't feel guilty about what he did next. Before Ace could do anything, Sincere emptied the rest of the clip into his body.

Boc. Boc. Boc. Boc

When the first bullet was fired, Ace flew back into the wall, dropping to the floor. Blood gushed out of Ace's mouth as he fought to save his life. Sincere ran over to Yana's lifeless body and held her.

"Baby, I'm so sorry that this happened to you," Sincere cried.

He looked over at Ace, who was still gasping for air.

"He-help me," Ace gasped.

"You deserve to die a slow and painful death. You ain't shit, Ace. I've always tried to help you, and this is how you repay me? I hope you rot in hell, you bastard," Sincere snapped as he spit on Ace.

Chelsea stood there with her gun in hand. She was shaking because she didn't know what to do next.

"Wh-where the fuck is the money," Chelsea stuttered.

Sincere looked at her, and he could see right through her. She was a female version of Ace.

"I could kill you right now, you stupid bitch. All this over money and revenge?" Sincere said.

Chelsea didn't respond. As time went on, Ace could no longer hold on. Sincere watched his brother die, but it didn't faze him. Throughout his entire life Ace envied him, and he could never understand why. When Ace killed Yana, he took a part of Sincere's heart. Sincere knew Ace was a fucked up individual, but he never thought he would have gone this far. This whole situation proved to Sincere that just because you had the same blood running through your veins, that didn't make you family.

Seventeen

Sarah was about to start cooking dinner. Something about that night just didn't feel right to her, and she knew something was wrong.

"Jason, I'll be back. I'm going to see if my sister is ok," Sarah told him.

"Wait, what's wrong?" Jason asked in concern.

"I don't know, but I just have this feeling that something's wrong with Yana. Since we were kids, we could always feel when the other one was in trouble, and right now I have that feeling," Sarah explained.

Jason understood, and he got baby Chelsea and put her in her car seat.

"Well, you're not going alone," Jason stated.

Sarah kissed him gently. She loved how he was there for her without a doubt.

"Ok. Well, let's get going, because she lives in Hopewell, and that's about an hour drive," Sarah told him.

They put baby Chelsea in the car and they were on their way. Sarah and Jason had no clue what they were about to face.

Eighteen

As they got closer to Sincere and Yana's house, they saw flashing lights.

"Oh my god, Jason, hurry up and stop the car!" Sarah screamed.

Jason was in a panic when he saw all of the police cars and ambulances. He stopped the car, and Sarah hopped out. Sincere was walking out of the house, and Sarah ran up to him.

"Sincere, what happened?" she asked in a frantic tone.

By the tears coming down Sincere's face, Sarah knew something was wrong.

"He killed Yana. Ace killed Yana," Sincere confessed as he broke down again.

"No!" Sarah screamed as she dropped to her knees.

When Jason saw Sarah drop to her knees, he quickly got out of the car. He ran to her side to comfort her.

"What happened, my love?" Jason asked.

"Ace killed Yana. Jason, he killed my sister," Sarah cried.

Jason's heart broke for her, but that wasn't the end of it. Jason's eyes grew wide when he saw Chelsea being brought out of the house in handcuffs. When their eyes connected, Chelsea put her head down in shame.

"Chelsea," Jason called out.

Sarah's head shot up when she heard that name. She looked at her and automatically assumed she had something to do with it. Sarah charged Chelsea and began to wail on her. Jason and a few of the officers ran to break things up.

"Sarah, stop it. You're going to get arrested, sweetheart, please stop," Jason begged.

"Sir, if you don't get her out of here, we will arrest her," one of the officers stated seriously.

"Sarah, we have to go. Baby Chelsea is in the car, so we have to go now," Jason said, hoping that when she heard Chelsea was in the car she would stop.

She soon stopped, and Jason was able to carry her to the car. When they got in the car, he checked on baby Chelsea, making sure she was ok. He thanked God he wasn't arrested for leaving her in the car unattended.

"Listen, I am going to drop you and Chelsea off, and then I am going to go to the police station to figure out what happened," Jason explained.

Sarah was too busy sobbing because of her sister's sudden death. She knew something had went on, but she never knew it was this bad. Sarah had lost a part of herself, and she didn't know how she was going to move on from this point.

Nineteen

After Jason dropped Sarah and baby Chelsea off, he headed back to the police station in Hopewell, New Jersey. When Jason got there, he didn't know what to think. He knew that once again Chelsea had gotten caught up.

"Sincere, what happened?" Jason asked.

Sincere looked up at Jason with red, puffy eyes. Jason could tell he had still been crying.

"Ace and an old friend of his named Rock tried to rob me. Me and Rock started tussling for the gun, and when I got ahold of the gun, I shot Rock. Next thing I knew, Ace blew Yana's brains out," Sincere explained through a cracked voice.

"How did Chelsea get involved?" Jason was eager to know.

"Man, I don't know. I've never even seen that girl before," Sincere said honestly.

Jason couldn't believe this happened. He knew Chelsea was going down. Jason took it upon himself to call Chelsea's parents. Jason knew damn well he was pushing his luck, because Chelsea's parents gave up on her a long time ago, but she needed them right now.

Twenty

It shocked Jason when Chelsea's parents came, but he was glad they did.

"Where is my daughter?" Roger asked.

Madalyn stood there in her fur coat not saying a word. Although she was just in a police station, her nose was still turned up.

"Roger, I'm so glad you came. Right now Chelsea is in custody. They're not letting me talk to her," Jason explained.

"I'm calling my lawyer," Roger said sternly.

"You most certainly are not. Chelsea got herself into this, and now she must get herself out of it," Madalyn said with attitude.

Both Roger and Jason looked at her. Now it was clear to Jason who let Chelsea go. It was her mother, and she wasn't afraid to let it be known.

"Madalyn, I refuse to let you continue to ruin me and my daughters' relationship. Chelsea needs us, and we're going to be there for her. It's bad enough when she contacted us for help years ago you turned her down. Now look what she's caught up in," Roger stated.

"If anything, Madalyn, Chelsea needs all of us. She's been feeling alone, and I think us being there as her support system will cause her to open her eyes and get clean," Jason admitted.

Madalyn wasn't for helping Chelsea at all. Chelsea could have been anything in the world, but she decided to choose the streets. Chelsea got hooked on drugs in college. When her parents found out, they immediately put her in rehab. After she was released from rehab, they thought Chelsea was clean, but when her twenty-first birthday came around, she clearly proved all of them wrong. Madalyn couldn't deal with Chelsea giving their family a bad name, so she put her out.

"I'm calling my driver. I will not be involved in this," Madalyn said as she took out her cell.

Roger snatched the phone out of her hand and slammed it down on the floor.

"For once, Madalyn, have a heart. This is our daughter we're talking about. All you've done was turn your back on her, but not this time. I won't let you," Roger said.

For the first time in five years, Madalyn broke down.

"I can't take this, Roger. Do you know how much this hurts me? My daughter is a drug addict and a prostitute," Madalyn cried.

Roger and Jason hugged her. This was hard for all of them, but right now they couldn't break down and be weak. They needed to be Chelsea's backbone.

"I understand how you feel. It was hard for me to witness certain things, but Chelsea needs us, and most of all she needs you, Madalyn," Jason explained.

Madalyn thought on it for a second. She knew this was going to be a hard process, but she also knew sometimes things got worse before they got better. She prayed and hoped this would be a true eye-opener for her daughter.

Twenty-One

A Month Later

Chelsea was released from jail, and she had to go to rehab. Although Chelsea had a terrible past and a record a mile long, her parents made sure her recent charges were dropped and never heard of again. Jason was doing all he could for Chelsea, and Sarah didn't like that at all.

"Where were you? I tried calling you, but I got no answer. Chelsea needs more milk," Sarah said.

Jason sat down and rubbed his eyes.

"I was at the rehab center, visiting Chelsea," Jason confessed.

Sarah looked at Jason with rage in her eyes.

"Jason, are you serious? It's been a month since my sister was murdered and you're already visiting her? Jason, how could you?" Sarah said, hurt.

"Sweetie, all I did was visit her. There is nothing going on between me and Chelsea," Jason explained.

"I didn't ask you if something was going on between you and Chelsea. I just can't believe my sister has been dead for only a month now and you are speaking to her as if she had nothing to do with it," Sarah said to him.

Jason understood how Sarah felt, but he had to explain to her that she couldn't blame Chelsea for what happened.

"Baby, please stop acting as if Chelsea is the devil. She had nothing to do with Yana's death. I understand she was there, but Ace killed Yana. Sarah, baby, I know all of this is hard, and I know you may think that I am a fool for helping Chelsea, but Chelsea and I will always have a friendship because of baby Chelsea," Jason explained.

Sarah ignored everything Jason said. She was hurt he was still associating with someone who played a part in her sister's death. Sarah felt as though Chelsea should've been behind bars. Nothing could bring her sister back, and the fact that everyone was on Chelsea's side made her feel like it was her against the world.

Twenty-Two

S incere was still taking the loss of his wife hard, but as each day went on, he tried to become at peace with everything. It was hard for Sincere to explain the situation to his fifteen-year-old son, Sincere Jr. He had to be strong for the both of them, but it wasn't easy. This was the first day Sincere would be confronting Chelsea about everything that happened. The rehabilitation center didn't allow visits on Sundays, but Sincere didn't care.

"I'm here to see Chelsea White," Sincere said when he walked up to the front desk.

"Sir, there are no visits allowed on Sundays," the lady at the front desk said to him.

"I understand that, but she's expecting me. I already talked to Mr. Kennedy, and this visit had already been approved," Sincere explained.

The lady said no more. She gave Sincere a pass and he headed in. Sincere waited outside for Chelsea. It took her about 10 minutes to come out, but when she did, she stopped in her tracks.

"You don't have to be afraid. I'm coming in peace. All I want to do is talk," Sincere assured her.

Chelsea looked back to make sure security was standing nearby, and Sincere caught on.

"Look here, sweetie, ain't nobody got time to be trying to hurt someone. Believe me, if I was going to do anything to you, I would've popped you as soon as you came through those double doors. I have a son that needs me, so me being locked behind bars for killing you won't do me or him any justice," Sincere explained.

Chelsea was now convinced Sincere really did come in peace. She couldn't quite understand why he was here, though. She walked over and sat next to him on the bench.

"So, why are you here?" Chelsea asked.

Sincere cleared his throat before starting.

"I want to know why. Why and how did you get involved with my brother? Was all this really over Sarah being with Jason?" Sincere wanted to know.

Chelsea wished she could forget all about that day. The image of Ace blowing Yana's head off replayed in her head as if it was a broken record.

"Is that something you really want to know?" Chelsea asked.

Sincere gave Chelsea a serious look, and that was all she needed to know he was serious.

"I met Ace a few years ago, at the age of 23 to be exact. He was on drugs, and so was I, so we instantly connected. I knew Ace was bad news, but having someone that understood my pain meant so much to me. I didn't know that Yana was Sarah's sister until that day. All of this was over money at first, but I can't lie. When I found out that they were sisters, I let my emotions get the best of me," Chelsea explained.

"So, you were mad that Sarah and Jason were together? But from what I heard, you didn't want to be with Jason. You chose the streets over love. So why the fuck are you mad?" Sincere snapped.

He was upset because Chelsea had no reason to be upset. She had ample chances to be with Jason, but instead she chose the street life. His wife got killed, and she didn't even have anything to do with what was going on. Yana didn't have anything to do with Ace and Sincere's beef, and she had nothing to do with Sarah and Jason's relationship.

"I know, and I shouldn't have let my emotions and feelings get the best of me. I just expected Jason to always take me back like he did before. I always wanted Jason to be happy because I knew I wasn't the woman for him. I am so sorry for what happened to your wife. No one was supposed to die that night. We never talked about that. All we wanted was the money," Chelsea explained.

Sincere looked at Chelsea as if she was a fool, but he also saw a little girl who was broken.

"What if there was no money? What if Ace was lying? You need to think before you act. Did Ace tell you that I worked my ass off for everything I got? Did he tell you how I've tried to check him into rehab and even give him a job? No, I bet he didn't tell you any of that. He was trying to make a quick come up, and he failed once again. Ace never wanted to work hard for anything. He always wanted a handout, and for some reason he felt as if the world owed him something," Sincere explained.

Chelsea listened to Sincere speak. She felt bad, because now that she was getting clean and her mind was functioning right, she had a chance to think about everything. The drugs had gotten her caught up, and now she was paying for it big time.

"You're right, and I feel so stupid for getting caught up in this. I know that there is nothing I can do to make things right, but if there was, what would it be?" Chelsea wanted to know.

Sincere thought on it for a second. He looked Chelsea directly in her eyes.

"Get clean, take care of your daughter, and never look your past in the eyes again," Sincere stated as he walked away.

It was weird to Chelsea that Sincere wasn't upset at her. He spoke nothing but truth to her. She refused to make any promise to a man, so she made a promise to God that she was going to get herself together and take care of her daughter. Drugs had taken over her life for far too long, and it was time to put an end to it.

Twenty-Three

J ason and Sarah were on bad terms. She was on the verge of leaving him, but baby Chelsea was holding her back. She grew to love that little girl so quickly, and there was nothing she could do about it. Sarah decided to move back into her old place in Hopewell. She was glad she didn't let it go, because she knew anything could've happened. Jason felt that he was losing Sarah, but he wasn't sure. He decided they needed to talk, so he arranged a nice candlelight dinner for the two of them.

"I'm glad you decided to show up. I was a bit worried that you wouldn't," Jason stated once Sarah arrived at his house.

She greeted him was a peck on the cheek.

"Where is Chelsea?" she asked as she sat down.

Jason pushed her chair in and took a seat himself.

"She's with Chelsea's mother," Jason revealed.

That was a shock to Sarah, considering everything she had heard about Chelsea and her parents not getting along.

"Oh, ok. Well, what are we eating?" Sarah asked.

Jason smiled as he removed the lids off the food.

"Well, you know steak is my favorite, so we're having that with grilled asparagus and tomatoes," he said to her.

Sarah nodded her head in approval. As they sat and ate, Sarah was very quiet. Jason felt some tension, so he decided to see what the problem was.

"Why are you so quiet?" Jason asked, breaking the silence.

Sarah put down her fork and looked at Jason. She felt a bit insulted that he acted as if he didn't know why there was tension in the air.

"Are you still in love with Chelsea?" Sarah said.

Jason was taken aback by the question she asked.

"Where is all of this coming from, Sarah?" Jason said.

"Jason, please cut the act. You know exactly where all of this is coming from. Now, please answer the question," Sarah said.

It took Jason a while to answer because he wasn't sure what to say. He loved Chelsea, but he wasn't in love with her like he used to be. All he wanted was for Chelsea to get clean, but he knew they would never work as a couple.

"Your silence is enough of an answer for me," Sarah said as she stood up.

"Sarah, wait," Jason called out to her.

When Sarah looked back, she had tears in her eyes.

"Jason, no. Your actions said enough. Do you think I wanted to come into this? I know you're still in love with Chelsea. That's why I didn't want to take our friendship to the next level, because I knew you weren't ready," Sarah stated.

Jason grabbed her by the hand. He couldn't risk losing her because he truly loved her.

"Sarah, I love you, and I want you to be in my life. I know that all of this is a lot. I'm sorry that your sister was murdered, I really am. If I could do anything to bring her back, I would, but you can't be upset with me because I still decide to help Chelsea. Yes, I love Chelsea, but I am not in love with her, nor can I be with her. Sarah, I love you, and only you. I love the relationship you and baby Chelsea have. I want to marry you, but if you don't trust me, how can I do that?" Jason said to her.

Sarah didn't know what to say. Since Yana died it seemed like her whole world went crashing down. All she wanted was her sister back. She was upset with Chelsea because she was there, but she couldn't blame her for Yana's death. Sarah loved Jason, and she didn't want to ruin things between them, but it was very hard for her.

"I just don't know what to do. A part of me wants to be mad at Chelsea because she was involved, but then a part of me knows she had nothing to do with the killing. Then here you are helping her as if nothing happened. I mean, hasn't she's done enough?" Sarah said.

Jason understood where she was coming from.

"I know, sweetie, I know. But Chelsea needs me. As a matter of fact, she needs all the help she can get. I know Chelsea has done a lot, but she also has a daughter that needs to know who her mother is when the time comes. I know you love baby Chelsea, so help me help her mother so that we can get past this and never look back," Jason explained.

Sarah knew Jason was right. It was a hard pill to swallow, but she loved Jason, and he loved her back. Yana's death was still hitting her hard, but she knew her sister would've wanted her to be the bigger person in this situation.

Twenty-Four

A few weeks went by, and Sarah stuck to her word. She was helping Jason help Chelsea get on the right path.

"Sarah, I can't thank you enough for helping me. I know you may never like me, but I truly appreciate everything you have done for me," Chelsea stated.

Since Chelsea had been clean, she was starting to think a lot clearer now. She saw things for what they really were instead of what she wanted them to be. Sarah was a beautiful person inside and out, and most of all she was the perfect woman for Jason. At first Chelsea was upset Jason had moved on, but at the end of the day she couldn't blame him.

"I don't dislike you, nor do I hate you. I just feel like you got caught up. No matter how much I wanted to blame you for Yana's death, I can't. All I want from this point on is for you to be Chelsea's mother. The streets don't love nobody, and you need to always remember that," Sarah spoke honestly.

Chelsea agreed. She didn't know how much love and care she really had until now.

"I'm thankful for everyone who has tried to help me," Chelsea said to her.

"We learn something from everyone who passes through our lives. Some lessons are painful, some are painless, but all are priceless," Sarah stated.

Twenty-Five

Between work and taking care of Sincere Jr., Sincere was beat. He didn't mind it at all because he knew his son needed him. The house without Yana was quiet, but he could still feel her presence. While Sincere was working, he would either send Sincere Jr. to his friend's house or over to Ms. Martha's house next door. She was a nice old lady, and when she found out about Yana being killed, she promised Sincere that if he ever needed anything, just call her.

"Sincere, are you hungry?" Sincere called out.

When he didn't get an answer, he ran upstairs to his room. When he opened his door, Sincere Jr. was sitting on the edge of his bed looking at a picture of Yana. He sat down beside his son.

"Are you ok?" he asked.

"Yeah, dad, I'm ok. It's just hard because mom would always cook us dinner, and mom would always come to my games. Now I don't have that anymore," Sincere Jr. explained.

"I feel you, and it's hard, but things will get better. Your mother is our guardian angel now," Sincere stated.

Sincere Jr. was quiet for a moment.

"Dad, will you ever date again? I know no one will ever replace mom, but I don't want you to be lonely," Sincere Jr. said.

That was really a shock to Sincere. His son was way more intelligent that he thought.

"Well, to be honest, I don't know. I mean, as of now it's way too soon to think about any of that. However, when the time comes for me to start dating, then I'll do it, but right now my only focus is you and being the best father I can be," Sincere responded.

Sincere didn't know where that question came from all of a sudden, but he was glad his son asked. They were close, but now that Yana was gone, Sincere wanted them to become closer. The hardest part about raising Sincere Jr. on his own was making sure the streets didn't get ahold of him.

Twenty-Six

When Chelsea found out Jeremy had turned himself in, she was shocked, but happy at the same time. She had to confront the man who almost took her life. She needed to know why he did that to her. It'd been a few months since she was checked into rehab, and she was ready to let go of all the burdens. Confronting Jeremy was something she needed to do. Chelsea sat there waiting for Jeremy to come out. She was nervous, but this was something she couldn't just sweep under the rug and move on from. When Jeremy came out, that was the first time Chelsea noticed how weak he actually was. He smiled when he saw her, but she didn't smile back.

"Chelsea, my beautiful snow bunny," Jeremy said as he sat down.

Chelsea looked at him in disgust. She couldn't believe how he came out with a smile plastered on his face.

"Don't call me that, and furthermore, you shouldn't be smiling, because I didn't come to visit to see how you were doing. I came to ask why did you do this to me, huh? I want to know why," Chelsea said as she showed him the deep cut he left on her neck.

The smile on Jeremy's face instantly left. He regretted that day, and if he could take it back he would. Just like Chelsea, Jeremy was hooked on drugs. But he was hooked on two kinds of drugs, which were crack and love. He never intended on things going that far, but when it did, it was out of his control.

"Chelsea, I am sorry. I — I don't know what came over me," Jeremy stated.

Chelsea rolled her eyes and threw her hands up.

"Oh, come on, Jeremy. Is that all you have for me? The least you can do is be honest and tell me the truth. I deserve that much," Chelsea told him.

Jeremy looked around at where he was. He figured that considering he was going to be in here for the rest of his life, there was no reason to lie. The whole situation was eating him up inside.

"The drugs got to me. Not only that, but I had fallen in love with you, and I didn't know how to control myself. Once I found out that you were with my son, I completely flipped out, and one thing led to another. I just couldn't control myself," Jeremy confessed.

As she listened to Jeremy, Chelsea understood the drug addiction part. She knew being hooked on drugs could have a person doing things they never thought they would ever do. The one thing that did puzzle her was when he said he found out about her being with his son.

"Wait a minute, your son? Derrick is your son?" Chelsea asked in shock.

Jeremy nodded his head.

"He was my son, but unfortunately he was murdered a few months ago. I feel terrible about everything. If I would've left the streets alone, then maybe he would be alive today. I abandoned him and his mother. Now he's dead, and I can only imagine how my wife, Demetria, is doing. I haven't spoken to her since I left years ago," Jeremy explained.

Chelsea was at a loss for words. She couldn't believe Derrick was murdered, but then again she could. Derrick was an evil person, and once he got ahold of someone, there was no turning back. Now that Chelsea looked back at everything that happened, she would've never gotten away from Derrick.

"I'm sorry for your loss. It's time for me to go now," Chelsea said as she stood up to leave.

"Chelsea, please don't leave just yet. You're the only person that came to visit me since I've been here. I don't want to go through this alone," Jeremy pleaded.

Chelsea turned around and looked at Jeremy as if he was crazy.

"Jeremy, I only came here to find out why you did this to me, but now that I know, I can erase you from my memory and my past. I was going to confront Derrick one day, but now that he's dead, I can't. Everything happens for a reason, and you can either let it break you or make you stronger. Well, I'm letting this make me stronger, and I refuse to look my past in its eyes again. So, with that being said, goodbye, Jeremy," Chelsea said as she walked out.

When Chelsea got outside, Sincere was waiting on her.

"How did it go?" he asked when she got into the car.

"It feels like a weight has been lifted off of my shoulders. He told me that Derrick was murdered a few months back, and the drugs and him being in love with me got the best of him. So he reacted off of emotions," Chelsea explained.

Sincere shook his head. He felt like Ace reacted off of emotions, but he wished it hadn't ended like that.

"So, do you forgive him?" Sincere asked.

Chelsea looked at him.

"Do you forgive me and Ace?" Chelsea asked.

Sincere sighed loudly.

"I forgive you, but me forgiving Ace is going to take some time because he was my brother, and he let his greed get the best of him," Sincere stated.

"Why do you forgive me?" Chelsea wanted to know.

"Because you're just a little girl lost in this big world. You're easily manipulated, and I feel like I could help you become a better person. Am I still hurt that you were there during the robbery? Yes, I am, but that wasn't the real Chelsea. That was the Chelsea that was high off of drugs," Sincere responded.

It made Chelsea smile that Sincere was willing to help her. She had lost Jason once due to her drug habit, and she refused to lose anyone else.

"Thank you. I needed to hear that. You know, it's pretty weird that I started out ratchet, and now I am growing into a beautiful woman," Chelsea said with a laugh.

"It's never too late to grow up and make a change. Always remember that," Sincere said.

Twenty-Seven

Tiffany had finally gotten her life back on track, and she was glad that she had. It was hard because she was still afraid she might get caught for what she did, but after praying and repenting, she felt like a new person. Tiffany had big dreams and goals, and now a baby on the way. When she found out she was pregnant, she cried for days. She thought about getting an abortion because she didn't know who the father was, but after giving it some thought, she decided to keep her child.

"Look at that baby bump," Rachel said with a smile.

Rachel was Tiffany's mother. At first they didn't get along, but after Rachel found out about what happened to Tiffany, she was heartbroken. Now, Rachel wasn't the best mother either, but she didn't have a drug addiction. She had a gambling addiction, and that ruined her relationship with her daughter.

Since Tiffany came back into her life, Rachel promised she was done with gambling. Her daughter needed her, and she needed her daughter. Tiffany believed her mother because their relationship had gotten better.

"Yeah, I can't wait until I find out what I'm having," Tiffany said excitedly.

Rachel started crying.

"Mom, what's wrong?" Tiffany asked in concern.

"Baby, you don't know how sorry I am. I just wish that I was a better mother to you because none of this would've happened," Rachel cried.

Tiffany hugged her mother tight. She felt as though they were both in the wrong. Instead of talking about the situation and finding out a solution, they both ran away from the problem.

"Mom, this is not your fault, and I don't blame you one bit. Things happen, and this was a lesson learned for the both of us," Tiffany responded.

Rachel wiped her tears and hugged her daughter back. She knew this was going to be a long journey to mend what was broken, but she was more than ready. All families go through things, but real family get through things.

Epilogue

ONE YEAR LATER

"Excuse me, is there something you want," she asked as she wiped her face.

"I'm just tryna figure out why a beautiful snow bunny like you out here at the bus stop alone. Where yo' man at, baby?" the guy asked her.

Chelsea looked up at the guy. It was déjà vu all over again, and before she knew it she was in his apartment having sex with him and eight of his friends for money.

***

Chelsea had just finished taking a hot shower. As she thought about her past, she looked in the mirror and smiled, because all of that was now over. She couldn't have been happier. Chelsea wrapped the towel around herself and walked into the bedroom. She crawled onto the bed and lay beside her man. He hugged her tight, and for the first time in her life she felt safe.

"So, I finally passed my twelve-month rehab program, and my daughter is coming to stay with us for the summer," Chelsea said with excitement.

"Baby, didn't I tell you that everything would fall into place? All you needed to do was change for the better. God heard your cries, and now he is answering your prayers," Sincere said as he kissed her on the forehead.

Chelsea smiled because he was right. Sincere was with her every step of the way, and she was thankful. When they first got together, she was nervous, but after a few months of dating Chelsea realized he was the best thing that ever happened to her. She thought his son, Sincere Jr., would probably hate her, but he didn't. Chelsea told Sincere Jr. everything from the beginning to the end. For a 16-year-old, he was more than understanding. Life was really going well for Chelsea. She was beyond thankful for each new challenge that had happened in her life because it helped build her strength and character.

***

Jason and Sarah were both doing great as newlyweds. Neither Jason nor Sarah was too excited about Chelsea and Sincere being together, but they finally grew to accept it. At first Sarah was hurt because she thought Sincere had betrayed her sister, but after having a long talk with him she understood the situation better. No matter whom Sincere was with, Yana would always hold a special place in his heart. However, they couldn't focus on Sincere and Chelsea's life because Sarah was expecting her first child with Jason. Jason was more than excited.

"So, are you ok with Chelsea going to stay with her mother for the summer?" Jason asked.

Sarah wobbled around the kitchen.

"Of course I am. They need to be closer, and Chelsea is clean, and she has been for a while. I feel like it's a great idea, and you know Sincere ain't gon' let nothing happen to her in his care," Sarah stated.

"Yeah, I still can't believe they're together. It's just one of those things that you never think would happen," Jason stated.

Sarah came and wrapped her arms around Jason and kissed him on the neck.

"Baby, I was surprised as well, but now that I think about it, I'm glad they're together. Sincere is a good man, and I know for a fact that Chelsea is in good hands. Everyone makes mistakes, but you have to learn to forgive and move on," Sarah explained.

Jason agreed. He was happy that Chelsea was happy. Sometimes he didn't understand why she couldn't be happy with him, but as he looked back on everything, he was glad things played out the way they did, because he found the love of his life. Sarah was everything and then some, and he could see himself spending the rest of his life with her.

"I guess that saying is true. Sometimes things get worse before they get better," Jason said with a chuckle.

*L*ife is what you make it. It's full of tough challenges, but as the saying goes, God gives his hardest battles to his strongest soldiers. I guess I was one of those strong soldiers. There will be all types of people who come in and out of your life, but you have to determine whether they are a blessing or a lesson. I've had a lot of lessons along the way, but that's ok, because now I have my blessings and lots of them. I know people may read my story and say I don't deserve happiness, and hey, I thought that, too. But I've learned that if God can forgive us and constantly give us second chances, then why can't I get a second chance? I know for a fact that I can't change my past, but I can change my future. I have failed many times in life, and I have done things in my past that I am not proud of, but my past is a part of me. It does not and it never will define me and who I am.

–Chelsea White

Reds Johnson also known as Anne Marie, is a twenty-three-year-old independent author born and raised in New Jersey. She started writing at the age of nine years old, and ever since then, writing has been her passion. Her inspirations were Danielle Santiago, and Wahida Clark. Once she came across their books; Reds pushed to get discovered around the age of thirteen going on fourteen.

To be such a young woman, the stories she wrote hit so close to home for many. She writes urban, romance, erotica, bbw, and teen stories and each book she penned is based on true events; whether she's been through it or witnessed it. After being homeless and watching her mother struggle for many years, Reds knew that it was time to strive harder. Her passion seeped through her pores so she knew that it was only a matter of time before someone gave her a chance.

Leaping head first into the industry and making more than a few mistakes; Reds now has the ability to take control of her writing career. She is on a new path to success and is aiming for bigger and better opportunities.

Visit my website www.iamredsjohnson.com

MORE TITLES BY REDS JOHNSON

SILVER PLATTER HOE 6 BOOK SERIES

HARMONY & CHAOS 6 BOOK SERIES

    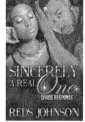

MORE TITLES BY REDS JOHNSON

NEVER TRUST A RATCHET BITCH 3 BOOK SERIES

TEEN BOOKS

A PROSTITUTE'S CONFESSIONS SERIES

CLOSED LEGS DON'T GET FED SERIES

MORE TITLES BY REDS JOHNSON

OTHER TITLES BY REDS JOHNSON

Made in the USA
Middletown, DE
17 August 2020

15186744R00060